Princesses Are Not Quitters!

For the real Allie and with thanks
to Libby and Meredith for being princesses – K.L.

For Alison – S.H.

First published in Great Britain in 2002 by Bloomsbury Publishing Plc
38 Soho Square, London, W1D 3HB
This paperback edition first published in 2003

A CIP catalogue record of this book is available from the British Library

ISBN 0 7475 6111 7

Printed in Hong Kong by South China Printing Co

10 9 8 7 6 5 4 3

Princesses Are Not Quitters!

Kate Lum

illustrated by Sue Hellard

ONCE there were three princesses: Princess Allie, Princess Mellie and Princess Libby. They lived in a huge silver palace by the sea with roses all around.

One morning they were sitting in the garden having breakfast when Princess Allie threw her toast on the ground.

"Oh I am so BORED!" she cried. "Being a princess is the dullest ever."

Just then, three servant girls walked by, carrying buckets of milk from the palace dairy.

"Just look at them," sighed Princess Libby. "Servants have all the fun!"

"Out in the fresh air, doing interesting things," said Princess Mellie.

Princess Allie jumped up, spilling her tea.

"Servant girls! Come here at once!" she cried.

The servants dropped their milk and rushed over.

"Give us those things you have on," ordered Princess Allie. "Put on our dresses instead. Now you can sit in the garden all day. Ha!"

The servant girls stared, but they did not argue.
They put on the silk dresses.
The princesses put on their rags,
and ran to the kitchen.

"Now, Mrs Blue," said Allie to the housekeeper, "today we princesses are going to be servants. From now until midnight, we want to be treated just like servants."

"Oh, ma'am, yes, Your Princesses,"
stammered Mrs Blue.
"But do you think that's a good idea, ma'am?"
"No arguing, Mrs Blue," said Libby.
So, Mrs Blue didn't argue.

"Well," she said, "if you are servants,
you're terribly late.
Work began four hours ago,
and you haven't done a thing."

"We're ready, Mrs Blue!" cried the princesses.
"Very well," said Mrs Blue, and she gave them a list of jobs.

“What fun, Mrs Blue!” cried the princesses, and they ran off to work.

They had to SWEEP the floors and

WHITEWASH the walls and

DUST the ceiling free of webs and

POLISH the windows and

SCRUB the pots and then go outside and

SWEEP the path and WEED the garden and

SCRUB the fountains and

FEED the hens and

PICK the cabbages for lunch and

… WASH the dogs and COMB the cats.

Very soon, Princess Mellie's back was sore, Princess Allie's hands were sore, and Princess Libby's feet were sore. But they didn't want anyone to say that Princesses are Quitters, so they kept on working.

Some of the jobs they couldn't do very well.

At last, however, they finished them all, and shuffled to the kitchen to find Mrs Blue.

"We're … all … finished … Mrs Blue," they panted. "We're ready … for … lunch."

"Lunch!" cried Mrs Blue. "Lunch? Lunch was over an hour ago and you're late with your afternoon work."

"AFTERNOON work?" groaned the princesses.

"Well of course," said Mrs Blue as she gave them another list of jobs.

This sounded like a lot of work to the princesses. But they didn't want anyone to say that Princesses are Quitters, so they hobbled outside and began.

They had to CHURN the butter and DRAIN the butter and MOLD the butter into pats and EVERY pat had to bear the crown to show that it's the royal kind and THEN

they had to MAKE the cheese

and PICK the fruit

and SWEEP the halls and BRING the water

and KNEAD the bread dough and PEEL the carrots

and SHEAR the sheep.

Some of the jobs they couldn't do very well. By the time they were finished, it was dark, and they staggered inside to find Mrs Blue.

“We’re … finished … Mrs Blue …” they puffed. “We’d … like … our dinners … now.”

“Dinner!” said Mrs Blue. “DINNER? Dinner was eaten two hours ago and you haven’t even started your evening chores!”

"EVENING CHORES!" cried the princesses.
"Well, yes," said Mrs Blue and she gave them yet more jobs.

The princesses were too tired to move. But they didn't want anyone to say that Princesses are Quitters. So they heaved themselves up and they dragged themselves out and they did all the jobs Mrs Blue had listed.

They had to SCRUB the pots and

SHINE the dishes and

THROW the water out the door and

WIPE the cups and

BAKE the bread and

PEEL the fruit for morning pie and THEN

they had to MILK the cows and
FEED them hay and

GET the eggs and
FEED the chickens
and WALK the dogs and

PET the cats and
LOCK the windows and
SNUFF the lights.

By the time they had finished it was midnight, Mrs Blue had gone to bed.

The princesses dragged themselves up the silver stairs and fell down snoring.
  The next day the princesses slept until noon. Then they bathed in tubs of rose water, and limped downstairs for breakfast.

"Say! I think … I made this bread!" said Allie.
"I peeled the fruit for this pie!" said Libby.
"I put the crown on this butter, see?" said Mellie.

As they sat there eating, the three servant girls walked by.
"How sore their backs must be," said Princess Mellie.
"How sore their hands must be," said Princess Allie.
"How sore their feet must be," said Princess Libby.
"Proclamation?" asked Princess Allie.
"Proclamation!" cried Libby and Mellie.

So they called on their page to blow the silver trumpet, and they climbed the silver stairs to the highest balcony.

When all the people had gathered, Princess Allie declared: "There will now be new rules for servants in this land. Things cannot go on as they are!"

The servants looked fearfully at each other.

"Here are the new rules!" cried Princess Libby.

"YOU HAVE TO …

SLEEP IN every day until nine and

WORK no more than you can do and

REST whenever you are tired and

EAT when you are hungry too

and SPEND an hour every day just SITTING in the gardens

and HAVE holidays every year

and let's have FUN!"

From that day to this, you will not find a happier princessdom than this one by the sea, but …

If you are looking for the princesses, don't try the garden. Try the dairy … the orchard … or the bakery, for …

Princesses are NOT Quitters!

NEVER QUIT